SPINOSAURUS
(SPINE-oh-SORE-us)

TYRANNOSAURUS REX
(tie-RAN-oh-sore-us rex)

APATOSAURUS
(ah-PAT-oh-sore-us)

VELOCIRAPTOR
(vel-OSS-ee-rap-tor)

To Rose and Harry, with love
T.K.

For Elin, the master of hide and seeks
S.W.

This edition published in the UK by Scholastic, 2022
1 London Bridge, London, SE1 9BA
Scholastic Ireland, 89E Lagan Road, Dublin Industrial Estate,
Glasnevin, Dublin, D11 HP5F
SCHOLASTIC and associated logos are trademarks and/or
registered trademarks of Scholastic Inc.

First published in the UK by Scholastic, 2015

Text © Timothy Knapman, 2015
Illustrations © Sarah Warburton, 2015

The moral rights of Timothy Knapman and Sarah Warburton have been asserted.

ISBN 978 0702 32305 8

Paper made from wood grown in sustainable forests and other controlled sources.

1 3 5 7 9 10 8 6 4 2

www.scholastic.co.uk

Dinosaurs
in my
School

Dinosaurs
in my
School

By Timothy Knapman

Illustrated by Sarah Warburton

SCHOLASTIC

There aren't any **dinosaurs** in my street —
I know, I'm not a fool.
You don't see a T. rex in the park
Or Iguanodons at the pool.
So tell me, please, oh why oh why...

Are there **dinosaurs** in my **school?**

SCHOOL

There's an Ankylosaur in the Art Room!
He's spraying paint around...

While the Hadrosaurs play silly games
With all the glitter they've found!

I try to make a picture,
But the moment that it's done...

Apatosaurus eats it
And my crayons, just for fun!

"There are dinosaurs in my school!" I say,
But the teachers just don't see.
When they find that dreadful mess
They're sure to think it's me.

I'll go and play some music…

No!

Stegosaurus got there first.
He broke the drums and tambourines
And his singing is the worst!

"Who has squashed the bookshelf?"
Our teacher asks us all.
"Someone's bitten the board in two!
There are claw marks on the wall!"

"There are DINOSAURS in our school!" I yell.
"We have to get them out!"
But Miss Brown says, "Sit still and shush.
It's not polite to shout."

There's no escape when it's time to eat.

A Pterosaur's pinched my food!
And when I say, "Hey, put that back!"
He makes a noise that's rude.

After lunch, we go outside
To run and jump and play,
But with all these naughty dinosaurs
There'll be no games today.

Triceratops pops footballs...

Velociraptor wins the race...

Spinosaurus steals the goal posts,
But the teachers won't give chase!

"Oh goodness me... Look!

DINOSAURS!

That boy was right!" they yelp,
And when they run away, I say,
"Will **somebody** please help?"

Our school is full of every kind
Of prehistoric creature!
But I know who will put things right
And that's our brave Head Teacher.

HEAD TEACHER

PLEASE KNOCK

So knocking gently on her door
I ask her what to do.
But when she comes to answer me...

She's a **dinosaur** too!

TRICERATOPS
(tri-SERRA-tops)

STEGOSAURUS
(STEG-oh-SORE-us)

PTEROSAUR
(TERR-oh-sore)

HADROSAURUS
(HAD-row-SORE-us)

ANKYLOSAURUS
(an-KIE-loh-sore-us)

PARASAUROLOPHUS
(pa-ra-saw-ROL-off-us)

IGUANODON
(ig-WHA-noh-don)

SPINOSAURUS
(SPINE-oh-SORE-us)

TYRANNOSAURUS REX
(tie-RAN-oh-sore-us rex)

APATOSAURUS
(ah-PAT-oh-sore-us)

VELOCIRAPTOR
(vel-OSS-ee-rap-tor)

Splat!